# THE BULL DOG BREED

## BY

## ROBERT E. HOWARD

**British Library Cataloguing-in-Publication Data**
A catalogue record for this book is available from the
British Library

# Robert E. Howard

Robert Ervin Howard was born in Peaster, Texas in 1906. During his youth, his family moved between a variety of Texan boomtowns, and Howard – a bookish and somewhat introverted child – was steeped in the violent myths and legends of the Old South. Although he loved reading and learning, Howard developed a distinctly Texan, hardboiled outlook on the world. He became a passionate fan of boxing, taking it up at an amateur level, and from the age of nine began to write adventure tales of semi-historical bloodshed. In 1919, when Howard was thirteen, his family moved to the Central Texas hamlet of Cross Plains, where he would stay for the rest of his life.

At fifteen Howard began to read the pulp magazines of the day, and to write more seriously. The December 1922 issue of his high school newspaper featured two of his stories, 'Golden Hope Christmas' and 'West is West'. In 1924 he sold his first piece – a short caveman tale titled 'Spear and Fang' – for $16 to the not-yet-famous *Weird Tales* magazine. He published with the magazine regularly over the next few years. 1929 was a breakout year for Howard, in that the 23-year-old writer began to sell to other magazines, such as *Ghost Stories* and *Argosy*, both of whom had previously sent him hundreds of rejection slips. In 1930, he began a correspondence with weird fiction master H. P. Lovecraft which ran up to his death six years later, and is regarded as one of the great correspondence cycles in all of fantasy literature.

It was partly due to Lovecraft's encouragement that Howard created his most famous character, Conan the Cimmerian. Conan – a barbarian-turned-King during the Hyborian Age, a mythical period of some 12,000 years ago – featured in seventeen *Weird Tales* stories between 1933 and 1936, and is now regarded as having spawned the 'sword and sorcery' genre, making Howard's influence on fantasy literature comparable to that of J. R. R. Tolkien's. The Conan stories have since been adapted many times, most famously in the series of films starring Arnold Schwarzenegger.

Howard was enjoying an all-time high in sales by the beginning of 1936, but he was also deeply upset by the ill health of his mother, who had fallen into a coma. On the morning of June 11, 1936, he asked an attending nurse whether she would ever recover, and the nurse replied negatively. Howard walked to his car, parked outside the family home in Cross Plains, and shot himself. He died eight hours later, aged just thirty.

"AND SO," CONCLUDED the Old Man, "this big bully ducked the seltzer bottle and the next thing I knowed I knowed nothin'. I come to with the general idee that the *Sea Girl* was sinkin' with all hands and I was drownin'—but it was only some chump pourin' water all over me to bring me to. Oh, yeah, the big French cluck I had the row with was nobody much, I learned—just only merely nobody but Tiger Valois, the heavyweight champion of the French navy—"

Me and the crew winked at each other. Until the captain decided to unburden to Penrhyn, the first mate, in our hearing, we'd wondered about the black eye he'd sported following his night ashore in Manila. He'd been in an unusual bad temper ever since, which means he'd been acting like a sore-tailed hyena. The Old Man was a Welshman, and he hated a Frenchman like he hated a snake. He now turned on me.

"If you was any part of a man, you big mick ham," he said bitterly, "you wouldn't stand around and let a blankety-blank French so-on and so-forth layout your captain. Oh, yeah, I know you wasn't there, then, but if you'll fight him—"

"Aragh!" I said with sarcasm, "leavin' out the fact that I'd stand a great chance of gettin' matched with Valois—why not pick me somethin' easy, like Dempsey? Do you realize you're askin' me, a ordinary ham-an'-egger, to climb the

3

original and only Tiger Valois that's whipped everything in European and the Asian waters and looks like a sure bet for the world's title?"

"Gerahh!" snarled the Old Man. "Me that's boasted in every port of the Seven Seas that I shipped the toughest crew since the days of Harry Morgan—" He turned his back in disgust and immediately fell over my white bulldog, Mike, who was taking a snooze by the hatch. The Old Man give a howl as he come up and booted the innocent pup most severe. Mike instantly attached hisself to the Old Man's leg, from which I at last succeeded in prying him with a loss of some meat and the pants leg.

The captain danced hither and yon about the deck on one foot while he expressed his feelings at some length and the crew stopped work to listen and admire.

"And get me right, Steve Costigan," he wound up, "the *Sea Girl* is too small for me and that double-dash dog. He goes ashore at the next port. Do you hear me?"

"Then I go ashore with him," I answered with dignity. "It was not Mike what caused you to get a black eye, and if you had not been so taken up in abusin' me you would not have fell over him.

"Mike is a Dublin gentleman, and no Welsh water rat can boot *him* and get away with it. If you want to banish your best A.B. mariner, it's up to you. Till we make port you keep your boots off of Mike, or I will personally kick you loose from your spine. If that's mutiny, make the most of it—and, Mister First Mate, I see you easin' toward that belayin' pin on the rail, and I call to your mind what I done to the last man that hit me with a belayin' pin."

There was a coolness between me and the Old Man thereafter. The old nut was pretty rough and rugged, but good at heart, and likely he was ashamed of himself, but he was too stubborn to admit it, besides still being sore at me and Mike. Well, he paid me off without a word at Hong Kong, and I went down the gangplank with Mike at my heels, feeling kind of queer and empty, though I wouldn't show it for nothing, and acted like I was glad to get off the old tub. But since I growed up, the *Sea Girl's* been the only home I knowed, and though I've left her from time to time to prowl around loose or to make a fight tour, I've always come back to her.

Now I knowed I couldn't come back, and it hit me hard. The *Sea Girl* is the only thing I'm champion of, and as I went ashore I heard the sound of Mushy Hansen and Bill O'Brien trying to decide which should succeed to my place of honor.

WELL, MAYBE SOME will say I should of sent Mike ashore and stayed on, but to my mind, a man that won't stand by his dog is lower down than one which won't stand by his fellow man.

Some years ago I'd picked Mike up wandering around the wharfs of Dublin and fighting everything he met on four legs and not averse to tackling two-legged critters. I named him Mike after a brother of mine, Iron Mike Costigan, rather well known in them higher fight circles where I've never gotten to.

Well, I wandered around the dives and presently fell in with Tom Roche, a lean, fighting engineer that I once knocked out in Liverpool. We meandered around, drinking here and there, though not very much, and presently found ourselves in a dump a little different from the general run. A French joint, kinda more highbrow, if you get me. A lot of swell-looking fellows was in there drinking, and the bartenders and waiters, all French, scowled at Mike, but said nothing. I was unburdening my woes to Tom, when I noticed a tall, elegant young man with a dress suit, cane and gloves stroll by our table. He seemed well known in the dump, because birds all around was jumping up from their tables and waving their glasses and yelling at him in French. He smiled back in a superior manner and flourished his cane in a way which irritated me. This galoot rubbed me the wrong way right from the start, see?

Well, Mike was snoozing close to my chair as usual, and, like any other fighter, Mike was never very particular where he chose to snooze. This big bimbo could have stepped over him or around him, but he stopped and prodded Mike with his cane. Mike opened one eye, looked up and lifted his lip in a polite manner, just like he was sayin': "We don't want no trouble; go 'long and leave me alone."

Then this French dipthong drawed back his patent leather shoe and kicked Mike hard in the ribs. I was out of my chair in a second, seeing red, but Mike was quicker. He shot up off the floor, not for the Frenchman's leg, but for his throat. But the Frenchman, quick as a flash, crashed his heavy cane down across Mike's head, and the bulldog hit the floor and laid still. The next minute the Frenchman hit the floor, and believe me he laid still! My right-hander to the jaw put him down, and the crack his head got against the corner of the bar kept him there.

I bent over Mike, but he was already coming around, in spite of the fact that a loaded cane had been broken over his head. It took a blow like that to put Mike out, even for a few seconds. The instant he got his bearings, his eyes went red and he started out to find what hit him and tear it up. I grabbed him, and for a minute it was all I could do to hold him. Then the red faded out of his eyes and he wagged his stump of a tail and licked my nose. But I knowed the first good chance he had at the Frenchman he'd rip out his throat or die trying. The only way you can lick a bulldog is to kill him.

Being taken up with Mike I hadn't had much time to notice what was going on. But a gang of French sailors had tried to rush me and had stopped at the sight of a gun in Tom Roche's hand. A real fighting man was Tom, and a bad egg to fool with.

By this time the Frenchman had woke up; he was standing with a handkerchief at his mouth, which latter was trickling blood, and honest to Jupiter I never saw such a pair of eyes on a human! His face was dead white, and those black, burning eyes blazed out at me—say, fellows!—they carried more than hate and a desire to muss me up! They was mutilation and sudden death! Once I seen a famous duelist in Heidelberg who'd killed ten men in sword fights—he had just such eyes as this fellow.

A gang of Frenchies was around him all whooping and yelling and jabbering at once, and I couldn't understand a word none of them said. Now one come prancing up to Tom Roche and shook his fist in Tom's face and pointed at me and yelled, and pretty soon Tom turned around to me and said: "Steve, this yam is challengin' you to a duel—what about?"

I thought of the German duelist and said to myself: "I bet this bird was born with a fencin' sword in one hand and a duelin' pistol in the other." I opened my mouth to say "Nothin' doin'—" when Tom pipes: "You're the challenged party—the choice of weapons is up to you."

At that I hove a sigh of relief and a broad smile flitted across my homely but honest countenance. "Tell him I'll fight him," I said, "with five-ounce boxin' gloves."

Of course I figured this bird never saw a boxing glove. Now, maybe you think I was doing him dirty, pulling a fast one like that—but what about him? All I was figuring on was mussing him up a little, counting on him not knowing a left hook from a neutral corner—takin' a mean advantage, maybe, but he was counting on killing me, and I'd never had a sword in my hand, and couldn't hit the side of a barn with a gun.

Well, Tom told them what I said and the cackling and gibbering bust out all over again, and to my astonishment I saw a cold, deadly smile waft itself across the sinister, handsome face of my tete-a-tete.

"They ask who you are," said Tom. "I told 'em Steve Costigan, of America. This bird says his name is Francois, which he opines is enough for *you*. He says that he'll fight you right away at the exclusive Napoleon Club, which it seems has a ring account of it occasionally sponsoring prize fights."

AS WE WENDED our way toward the aforesaid club, I thought deeply. It seemed very possible that this Francois, whoever he was, knew something of the manly art. Likely, I thought, a rich clubman who took up boxing for a hobby. Well, I reckoned he hadn't heard of me, because no amateur, however rich, would think he had a chance against Steve Costigan, known in all ports as the toughest sailor in the Asian waters—if I do say so myself—and champion of— what I mean—ex-champion of the *Sea Girl*, the toughest of all the trading vessels.

A kind of pang went through me just then at the thought that my days with the old tub was ended, and I wondered what sort of a dub would take my place at mess and sleep in my bunk, and how the forecastle gang would haze him, and how all the crew would miss me—I wondered if Bill O'Brien had licked Mushy Hansen or if the Dane had won, and who called hisself champion of the craft now—

Well, I felt low in spirits, and Mike knowed it, because he snuggled up closer to me in the 'rickshaw that was carrying us to the Napoleon Club, and licked my hand. I pulled his ears and felt better. Anyway, Mike wouldn't never desert me.

Pretty ritzy affair this club. Footmen or butlers or something in uniform at the doors, and they didn't want to let Mike in. But they did—oh, yeah, they did.

In the dressing room they give me, which was the swellest of its sort I ever see, and looked more like a girl's boodwar than a fighter's dressing room, I said to Tom: "This big ham must have lots of dough—notice what a hand they all give him? Reckon I'll get a square deal? Who's goin' to referee? If it's a Frenchman, how'm I gonna follow the count?"

"Well, gee whiz!" Tom said, "you ain't expectin' him to count over you, are you?"

"No," I said. "But I'd like to keep count of what he tolls off over the other fellow."

"Well," said Tom, helping me into the green trunks they'd give me, "don't worry none. I understand Francois can speak English, so I'll specify that the referee shall converse entirely in that language."

"Then why didn't this Francois ham talk English to me?" I wanted to know.

"He didn't talk to you in anything," Tom reminded me. "He's a swell and thinks you're beneath his notice—except only to knock your head off."

"H'mm," said I thoughtfully, gently touching the slight cut which Francois' cane had made on Mike's incredibly hard head. A slight red mist, I will admit, waved in front of my eyes.

When I climbed into the ring I noticed several things: mainly the room was small and elegantly furnished; second, there was only a small crowd there, mostly French, with a scattering of English and one Chink in English clothes. There was high hats, frock-tailed coats and gold-knobbed canes everywhere, and I noted with some surprise that they was also a sprinkling of French sailors.

I sat in my corner, and Mike took his stand just outside, like he always does when I fight, standing on his hind legs with his head and forepaws resting on the edge of the canvas, and looking under the ropes. On the street, if a man soaks me he's likely to have Mike at his throat, but the old dog knows how to act in the ring. He won't interfere, though sometimes when I'm on the canvas or bleeding bad his eyes get red and he rumbles away down deep in his throat.

TOM WAS MASSAGING my muscles light-like and I was scratching Mike's ears when into the ring comes Francois the Mysterious. *Oui! Oui!* I noted now how much of a man he was, and Tom whispers to me to pull in my chin a couple of feet and stop looking so goofy. When Francois threw off his silk embroidered bathrobe I saw I was in for a rough session, even if this bird was only an amateur. He was one of these fellows that *look* like a fighting man, even if they've never seen a glove before.

A good six one and a half he stood, or an inch and a half taller than me. A powerful neck sloped into broad, flexible shoulders, a limber steel body tapered to a girlishly slender waist. His legs was slim, strong and shapely, with narrow feet that looked speedy and sure; his arms was long, thick, but perfectly molded. Oh, I tell you, this Francois looked more like a champion than any man I'd seen since I saw Dempsey last.

And the face—his sleek black hair was combed straight back and lay smooth on his head, adding to his sinister good looks. From under narrow black brows them eyes burned at me, and now they wasn't a duelist's eyes—they was tiger eyes. And when he gripped the ropes and dipped a couple of times, flexing his muscles, them muscles rippled under his satiny skin most beautiful, and he looked just like a big cat sharpening his claws on a tree.

"Looks fast, Steve," Tom Roche said, looking serious. "May know somethin'; you better crowd him from the gong and keep rushin'—"

"How else did I ever fight?" I asked.

A sleek-looking Frenchman with a sheik mustache got in the ring and, waving his hands to the crowd, which was still jabbering for Francois, he bust into a gush of French.

"What's he mean?" I asked Tom, and Tom said, "Aw, he's just sayin' what everybody knows—that this ain't a regular prize fight, but an affair of honor between you and—uh—that Francois fellow there."

Tom called him and talked to him in French, and he turned around and called an Englishman out of the crowd. Tom asked me was it all right with me for the Englishman to referee, and I tells him yes, and they asked Francois and he nodded in a supercilious manner. So the referee asked me what I weighed and I told him, and he hollered: "This bout is to be at catch weights, Marquis of Queensberry rules. Three-minute rounds, one minute rest; to a finish, if it takes all night. In this corner, Monsieur Francois, weight 205 pounds; in this corner, Steve Costigan of America, weight 190 pounds. Are you ready, gentlemen?"

'Stead of standing outside the ring, English style, the referee stayed in with us, American fashion. The gong sounded and I was out of my corner. All I seen was that cold, sneering, handsome face, and all I wanted to do was to spoil it. And I very nearly done it the first charge. I came in like a house afire and I walloped Francois with an overhand right hook to the chin—more by sheer luck than anything, and it landed high. But it shook him to his toes, and the sneering smile faded.

TOO QUICK FOR the eye to follow, his straight left beat my left hook, and it packed the jarring kick that marks a puncher. The next minute, when I missed with both hands and got that left in my pan again, I knowed I was up against a master boxer, too.

I saw in a second I couldn't match him for speed and skill. He was like a cat; each move he made was a blur of speed, and when he hit he hit quick and hard. He was a brainy fighter—he thought out each move while traveling at high speed, and he was never at a loss what to do next.

Well, my only chance was to keep on top of him, and I kept crowding him, hitting fast and heavy. He wouldn't stand up to me, but back-pedaled all around the ring. Still, I got the idea that he wasn't afraid of me, but was retreating with a purpose of his own. But I never stop to figure out why the other bird does something.

He kept reaching me with that straight left, until finally I dived under it and sank my right deep into his midriff. It shook him—it should of brought him down. But he clinched and tied me up so I couldn't hit or do nothing. As the referee broke us Francois scraped his glove laces across my eyes. With an appropriate remark, I threw my right at his head with everything I had, but he drifted out of the way, and I fell into the ropes from the force of my own swing. The crowd howled with laughter, and then the gong sounded.

"This baby's tough," said Tom, back in my corner, as he rubbed my belly muscles, "but keep crowdin' him, get inside that left, if you can. And watch the right."

I reached back to scratch Mike's nose and said, "You watch this round."

Well, I reckon it was worth watching. Francois changed his tactics, and as I come in he met me with a left to the nose that started the claret and filled my eyes full of water and stars. While I was thinking about that he opened a cut under my left eye with a venomous right-hander and then stuck the same hand into my midriff. I woke up and bent him double with a savage left hook to the liver, crashing him with an overhand right behind the ear before he could straighten. He shook his head, snarled a French cuss word and drifted back behind that straight left where I couldn't reach him.

15

I went into him like a whirlwind, lamming head on full into that left jab again and again, trying to get to him, but always my swings were short. Them jabs wasn't hurting me yet, because it takes a lot of them to weaken a man. But it was like running into a floating brick wall, if you get what I mean. Then he started crossing his right—and oh, baby, what a right he had! Blip! Blim! Blam!

His rally was so unexpected and he hit so quick that he took me clean off my guard and caught me wide open. That right was lightning! In a second I was groggy, and Francois beat me back across the ring with both hands going too fast for me to block more than about a fourth of the blows. He was wild for the kill now and hitting wide open.

Then the ropes was at my back and I caught a flashing glimpse of him, crouching like a big tiger in front of me, wide open and starting his right. In that flash of a second I shot my right from the hip, beat his punch and landed solid to the button. Francois went down like he'd been hit with a pile driver—the referee leaped forward—the gong sounded!

As I went to my corner the crowd was clean ory-eyed and not responsible; and I saw Francois stagger up, glassy-eyed, and walk to his stool with one arm thrown over the shoulder of his handler.

But he come out fresh as ever for the third round. He'd found out that I could hit as hard as he could and that I was dangerous when groggy, like most sluggers. He was wild with rage, his smile was gone, his face dead white again, his eyes was like black fires—but he was cautious. He side-stepped my rush, hooking me viciously on the ear as I shot past him, and ducking when I slewed around and hooked my right. He backed away, shooting that left to my face. It went that way the whole round; him keeping the right reserved and marking me up with left jabs while I worked for his body and usually missed or was blocked. Just before the gong he rallied, staggered me with a flashing right hook to the head and took a crushing left hook to the ribs in return.

THE FOURTH ROUND come and he was more aggressive. He began to trade punches with me again. He'd shoot a straight left to my face, then hook the same hand to my body. Or he'd feint the left for my face and drop it to my ribs. Them hooks to the body didn't hurt much, because I was hard as a rock there, but a continual rain of them wouldn't do me no good, and them jabs to the face was beginning to irritate me. I was already pretty well marked up.

He shot his blows so quick I usually couldn't block or duck, so every time he'd make a motion with the left I'd throw my right for his head haphazard. After rocking his head back several times this way he quit feinting so much and began to devote most of his time to body blows.

Now I found out this about him: he had more claws than sand, as the saying goes. I mean he had everything, including a lot of stuff I didn't, but he didn't like to take it.

In a mix-up he always landed three blows to my one, and he hit about as hard as I did, but he was always the one to back away.

Well, come the seventh round. I'd taken plenty. My left eye was closing fast and I had a nasty gash over the other one. My ribs was beginning to feel the body punishment he was handing out when in close, and my right ear was rapidly assuming the shape of a cabbage. Outside of some ugly welts on his torso, my dancing partner had only one mark on him—the small cut on his chin where I'd landed with my bare fist earlier in the evening.

But I was not beginning to weaken for I'm used to punishment; in fact I eat it up, if I do say so. I crowded Francois into a corner before I let go. I wrapped my arms around my neck, worked in close and then unwound with a looping left to the head.

Francois countered with a sickening right under the heart and I was wild with another left. Francois stepped inside my right swing, dug his heel into my instep, gouged me in the eye with his thumb and, holding with his left, battered away at my ribs with his right. The referee showed no inclination to interfere with this pastime, so, with a hearty oath, I wrenched my right loose and nearly tore off Francois' head with a torrid uppercut.

His sneer changed to a snarl and he began pistoning me in the face again with his left. Maddened, I crashed into him headlong and smashed my right under his heart—I felt his ribs bend, he went white and sick and clinched before I could follow up my advantage. I felt the drag of his body as his knees buckled, but he held on while I raged and swore, the referee would not break us, and when I tore loose, my charming playmate was almost as good as ever.

He proved this by shooting a left to my sore eye, dropping the same hand to my aching ribs and bringing up a right to the jaw that stretched me flat on my back for the first time that night. Just like that! *Biff—bim—bam!* Like a cat hitting—and I was on the canvas.

Tom Roche yelled for me to take a count, but I never stay on the canvas longer than I have to. I bounced up at "Four!" my ears still ringing and a trifle dizzy, but otherwise O.K.

Francois thought otherwise, rushed rashly in and stopped a left hook which hung him gracefully over the ropes. The gong!

The beginning of the eighth I come at Francois like we'd just started, took his right between my eyes to hook my left to his body—he broke away, spearing me with his left—I followed swinging—missed a right—*crack!*

He musta let go his right with all he had for the first time that night, and he had a clear shot to my jaw. The next thing I knowed, I was writhing around on the canvas feeling like my jaw was tore clean off and the referee was saying: "—seven—"

Somehow I got to my knees. It looked like the referee was ten miles away in a mist, but in the mist I could see Francois' face, smiling again, and I reeled up at "nine" and went for that face. *Crack! Crack!* I don't know what punch put me down again but there I was. I beat the count by a hair's breadth and swayed forward, following my only instinct and that was to walk into him!

FRANCOIS MIGHT HAVE finished me there, but he wasn't taking any chances for he knowed I was dangerous to the last drop. He speared me a couple of times with the left, and when he shot his right, I ducked it and took it high on my forehead and clinched, shaking my head to clear it. The referee broke us away and Francois lashed into me, cautious but deadly, hammering me back across the ring with me crouching and covering up the best I could.

On the ropes I unwound with a venomous looping right, but he was watching for that and ducked and countered with a terrible left to my jaw, following it with a blasting right to the side of the head. Another left hook threw me back into the ropes and there I caught the top rope with both hands to keep from falling. I was swaying and ducking but his gloves were falling on my ears and temples with a steady thunder which was growing dimmer and dimmer—then the gong sounded.

I let go of the ropes to go to my corner and when I let go I pitched to my knees. Everything was a red mist and the crowd was yelling about a million miles away. I heard Francois' scornful laugh, then Tom Roche was dragging me to my corner.

"By golly," he said, working on my cut up eyes, "you're sure a glutton for punishment; Joe Grim had nothin' on you.

"But you better lemme throw in the towel, Steve. This Frenchman's goin' to kill you—"

"He'll have to, to beat me," I snarled. "I'll take it standin'."

"But, Steve," Tom protested, mopping blood and squeezing lemon juice into my mouth, "this Frenchman is—"

But I wasn't listening. Mike knowed I was getting the worst of it and he'd shoved his nose into my right glove, growling low down in his throat. And I was thinking about something.

One time I was laid up with a broken leg in a little fishing village away up on the Alaskan coast, and looking through a window, not able to help him, I saw Mike fight a big gray devil of a sled dog—more wolf than dog. A big gray killer. They looked funny together—Mike short and thick, bow-legged and squat, and the wolf dog tall and lean, rangy and cruel.

Well, while I lay there and raved and tried to get off my bunk with four men holding me down, that blasted wolf-dog cut poor old Mike to ribbons. He was like lightning—like Francois. He fought with the slash and get away—like Francois. He was all steel and whale-bone—like Francois.

Poor old Mike had kept walking into him, plunging and missing as the wolf-dog leaped aside—and every time he leaped he slashed Mike with his long sharp teeth till Mike was bloody and looking terrible. How long they fought I don't know. But Mike never give up; he never whimpered; he never took a single back step; he kept walking in on the dog.

At last he landed—crashed through the wolf-dog's defense and clamped his jaws like a steel vise and tore out the wolf-dog's throat. Then Mike slumped down and they brought him into my bunk more dead than alive. But we fixed him up and finally he got well, though he'll carry the scars as long as he lives.

And I thought, as Tom Roche rubbed my belly and mopped the blood off my smashed face, and Mike rubbed his cold, wet nose in my glove, that me and Mike was both of the same breed, and the only fighting quality we had was a everlasting persistence. You got to kill a bulldog to lick him. Persistence! How'd I ever won a fight? How'd Mike ever won a fight? By walking in on our men and never giving up, no matter how bad we was hurt! Always outclassed in everything except guts and grip! Somehow the fool Irish tears burned my eyes and it wasn't the pain of the collodion Tom was rubbing into my cuts and it wasn't self-pity—it was—I don't know what it was! My grandfather used to say the Irish cried at Benburb when they were licking the socks off the English.

THEN THE GONG sounded and I was out in the ring again playing the old bulldog game with Francois—walking into him and walking into him and taking everything he handed me without flinching.

I don't remember much about that round. Francois' left was a red-hot lance in my face and his right was a hammer that battered in my ribs and crashed against my dizzy head. Toward the last my legs felt dead and my arms were like lead. I don't know how many times I went down and got up and beat the count, but I remember once in a clinch, half-sobbing through my pulped lips: "You gotta kill me to stop me, you big hash!" And I saw a strange haggard look flash into his eyes as we broke. I lashed out wild and by luck connected under his heart. Then the red fog stole back over everything and then I was back on my stool and Tom was holding me to keep me from falling off.

"What round's this comin' up?" I mumbled.

"The tenth," he said. "For th' luvva Pete, Steve, quit!"

I felt around blind for Mike and felt his cold nose on my wrist.

"Not while I can see, stand or feel," I said, deliriously. "It's bulldog and wolf—and Mike tore his throat out in the end—and I'll rip this wolf apart sooner or later."

Back in the center of the ring with my chest all crimson with my own blood, and Francois' gloves soggy and splashing blood and water at every blow, I suddenly realized that his punches were losing some of their kick. I'd been knocked down I don't know how many times, but I now knew he was hitting me his best and I still kept my feet. My legs wouldn't work right, but my shoulders were still strong. Francois played for my eyes and closed them both tight shut, but while he was doing it I landed three times under the heart, and each time he wilted a little.

"What round's comin' up?" I groped for Mike because I couldn't see.

"The eleventh—this is murder," said Tom. "I know you're one of these birds which fights twenty rounds after they've been knocked cold, but I want to tell you this Frenchman is—"

"Lance my eyelid with your pocket-knife," I broke in, for I had found Mike. "I gotta see."

Tom grumbled, but I felt a sharp pain and the pressure eased up in my right eye and I could see dim-like.

Then the gong sounded, but I couldn't get up; my legs was dead and stiff.

"Help me up, Tom Roche, you big bog-trotter," I snarled. "If you throw in that towel I'll brain you with the water bottle!"

With a shake of his head he helped me up and shoved me in the ring. I got my bearings and went forward with a funny, stiff, mechanical step, toward Francois—who got up slow, with a look on his face like he'd rather be somewhere else. Well, he'd cut me to pieces, knocked me down time and again, and here I was coming back for more. The bulldog instinct is hard to fight—it ain't just exactly courage, and it ain't exactly blood lust—it's—well, it's the bulldog breed.

NOW I WAS facing Francois and I noticed he had a black eye and a deep gash under his cheek bone, though I didn't remember putting them there. He also had welts a-plenty on his body. I'd been handing out punishment as well as taking it, I saw.

Now his eyes blazed with a desperate light and he rushed in, hitting as hard as ever for a few seconds. The blows rained so fast I couldn't think and yet I knowed I must be clean batty—punch drunk—because it seemed like I could hear familiar voices yelling my name—the voices of the crew of the *Sea Girl*, who'd never yell for me again.

I was on the canvas and this time I felt that it was to stay; dim and far away I saw Francois and somehow I could tell his legs was trembling and he shaking like he had a chill. But I couldn't reach him now. I tried to get my legs under me, but they wouldn't work. I slumped back on the canvas, crying with rage and weakness.

Then through the noise I heard one deep, mellow sound like an old Irish bell, almost. Mike's bark! He wasn't a barking dog; only on special occasions did he give tongue. This time he only barked once. I looked at him and he seemed to be swimming in a fog. If a dog ever had his soul in his eyes, he had; plain as speech them eyes said: "Steve, old kid, get up and hit one more blow for the glory of the breed!"

I tell you, the average man has got to be fighting for somebody else besides hisself. It's fighting for a flag, a nation, a woman, a kid or a dog that makes a man win. And I got up—I dunno how! But the look in Mike's eyes dragged me off the canvas just as the referee opened his mouth to say "Ten!" But before he could say it—

In the midst I saw Francois' face, white and desperate. The pace had told. Them blows I'd landed from time to time under the heart had sapped his strength—he'd punched hisself out on me—but more'n anything else, the knowledge that he was up against the old bulldog breed licked him.

I drove my right smash into his face and his head went back like it was on hinges and the blood spattered. He swung his right to my head and it was so weak I laughed, blowing out a haze of blood. I rammed my left to his ribs and as he bent forward I crashed my right to his jaw. He dropped, and crouching there on the canvas, half supporting himself on his hands, he was counted out. I reeled across the ring and collapsed with my arms around Mike, who was whining deep in his throat and trying to lick my face off.

THE FIRST THING I felt on coming to, was a cold, wet nose burrowing into my right hand, which seemed numb. Then somebody grabbed that hand and nearly shook it off and I heard a voice say: "Hey, you old shellback, you want to break a unconscious man's arm?"

I knowed I was dreaming then, because it was Bill O'Brien's voice, who was bound to be miles away at sea by this time. Then Tom Roche said: "I think he's comin' to. Hey, Steve, can you open your eyes?"

I took my fingers and pried the swollen lids apart and the first thing I saw, or wanted to see, was Mike. His stump tail was going like anything and he opened his mouth and let his tongue loll out, grinning as natural as could be. I pulled his ears and looked around and there was Tom Roche—and Bill O'Brien and Mushy Hansen, Olaf Larsen, Penrhyn, the first mate, Red O'Donnell, the second—and the Old Man!

"Steve!" yelled this last, jumping up and down and shaking my hand like he wanted to take it off, "you're a wonder! A blightin' marvel!"

"Well," said I, dazed, "why all the love fest—"

"The fact is," bust in Bill O'Brien, "just as we're about to weigh anchor, up blows a lad with the news that you're fightin' in the Napoleon Club with—"

27

"—and as soon as I heard who you was fightin' with I stopped everything and we all blowed down there," said the Old Man. "But the fool kid Roche had sent for us loafed on the way—"

"—and we hadda lay some Frenchies before we could get in," said Hansen.

"So we saw only the last three rounds," continued the Old Man. "But, boy, they was worth the money—he had you outclassed every way except guts—you was licked to a frazzle, but he couldn't make you realize it—and I laid a bet or two—"

And blow me, if the Old Man didn't stuff a wad of bills in my sore hand.

"Halfa what I won," he beamed. "And furthermore, the *Sea Girl* ain't sailin' till you're plumb able and fit."

"But what about Mike?" My head was swimming by this time.

"A bloomin' bow-legged angel," said the Old Man, pinching Mike's ear lovingly. "The both of you kin have my upper teeth! I owe you a lot, Steve. You've done a lot for me, but I never felt so in debt to you as I do now. When I see that big French ham, the one man in the world I would of give my right arm to see licked—"

"Hey!" I suddenly seen the light, and I went weak and limp. "You mean that was—"

"You whipped Tiger Valois, heavyweight champion of the French fleet, Steve," said Tom. "You ought to have known how he wears dude clothes and struts amongst the swells when on shore leave. He wouldn't tell you who he was for fear you wouldn't fight him; and I was afraid I'd discourage you if I told you at first and later you wouldn't give me a chance."

"I might as well tell you," I said to the Old Man, "that I didn't know this bird was the fellow that beat you up in Manila. I fought him because he kicked Mike."

"Blow the reason!" said the Old Man, raring back and beaming like a jubilant crocodile. "You licked him—that's enough. Now we'll have a bottle opened and drink to Yankee ships and Yankee sailors—especially Steve Costigan."

"Before you do," I said, "drink to the boy who stands for everything them aforesaid ships and sailors stands for—Mike of Dublin, an honest gentleman and born mascot of all fightin' men!"

THE END